MAGGIE LI

THE AMAZING HUMAN
BODY DETECTIVES

FACTS, MYTHS AND QUIRKS OF THE BODY

PAVILION

CONTENTS

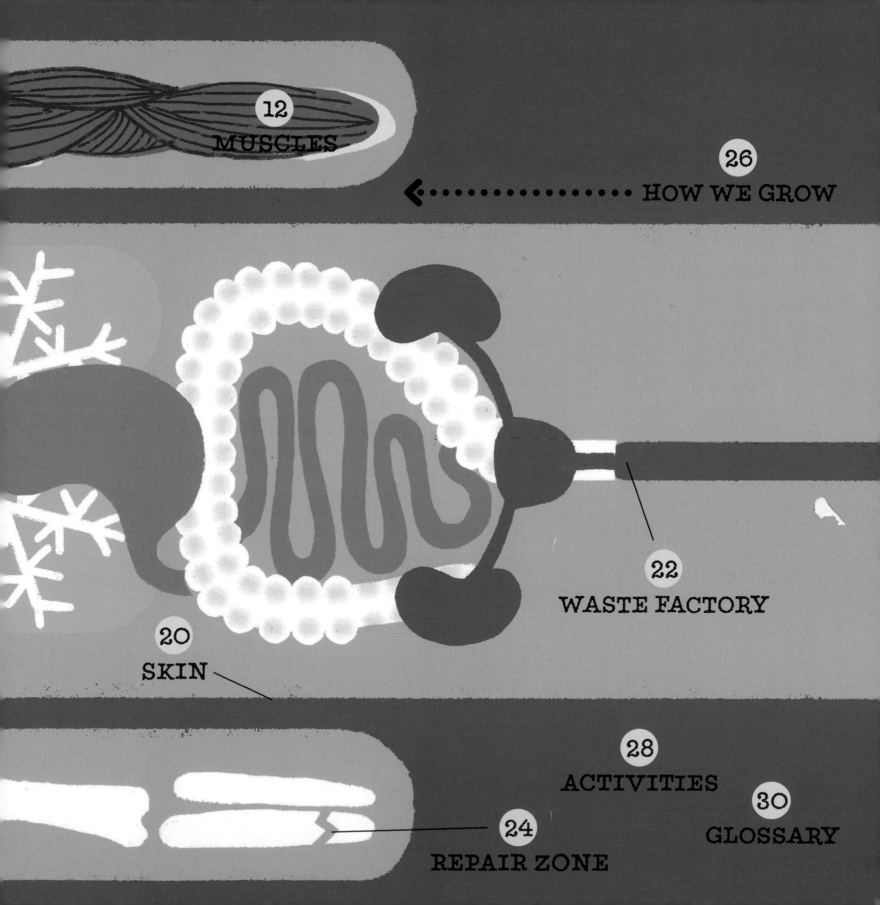

BUSY ORGANS

Your body is made up of some very important organs that keep you alive by circulating blood, oxygen and waste products to the right places. You would not be able to live without your heart, lungs or kidneys, so they need looking after. You can do this by exercising and eating healthily.

Your heart works hard and beats over 100,000 times a day.

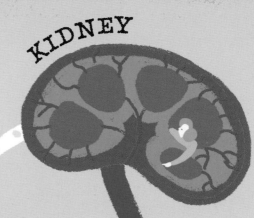

KIDNEY

LAUGH FACTORY

Ha ha! Ha ha! Ha ha! Ha ha! Ha ha! Ha ha! Ha ha! Ha ha! Ha ha!

Laughing is good for your heart, so get giggling!

The job of your kidneys is to filter all the nasties out of your blood into your wee. They work in a similar way to a sieve — like the ones you use when you're baking!

Platelets help your blood to clot.

White blood cells help fight infection in the body.

Red blood cells carry oxygen around the body.

BLOOD ZONE

Q Which bean do you think a kidney looks like?

A A kidney bean!

KIDNEY

Can you find the tanks of different blood cells being transported around the body?

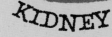

Use your magnifying glass to find the blood tanks!

HINT!
If you don't know where to find it, use your magnifying glass to find good pulse spots on the body!

BODY CHALLENGE

Try to find your own pulse and count it...

LUNGS

Your lungs are filled with over 300 million tiny air bags called alveoli. They transfer oxygen to your blood.

Your heart is the same size as your fist.

The heart has four chambers.

HEART

Your heart beats, or pulses, around 80-100 times a minute (normally). Try counting to 100 in a minute. Fast, isn't it?

Your lungs provide oxygen from the air you breathe in. Your heart then pumps blood carrying oxygen all around your body.

LUNGS

You breathe in 11,000 litres of air every day. That's enough to fill 5,500 bottles!

Your blood travels around your body carrying vital nutrients to different parts.

BLOOD HIGHWAY

TEETH AND BONES

Your bones support your body in a connecting framework called the skeleton. Your teeth help you cut and chew the food that you eat, making it easier for you to swallow and digest it.

Brushing your teeth helps to keep them healthy by removing bits of food that are hiding on the surface and between each tooth.

SKULL
This protects your brain.

Bones are the hardest things in your body. They support and protect you and make it possible for you to move around.

DID YOU KNOW?
Your funny bone isn't a bone at all! It is a nerve that lives in your elbow.

RIBCAGE
This protects some of your organs including your heart.

FUNNY BONES!
Can you find the laughing bones?

SPINE
This is made up of 33 smaller bones that help you stand up straight.

THE SKELETON

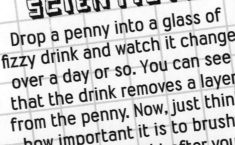

CALLING MINI SCIENTISTS

Drop a penny into a glass of fizzy drink and watch it change over a day or so. You can see that the drink removes a layer from the penny. Now, just think how important it is to brush your teeth at night after you have had a fizzy drink!

A CLOSER LOOK

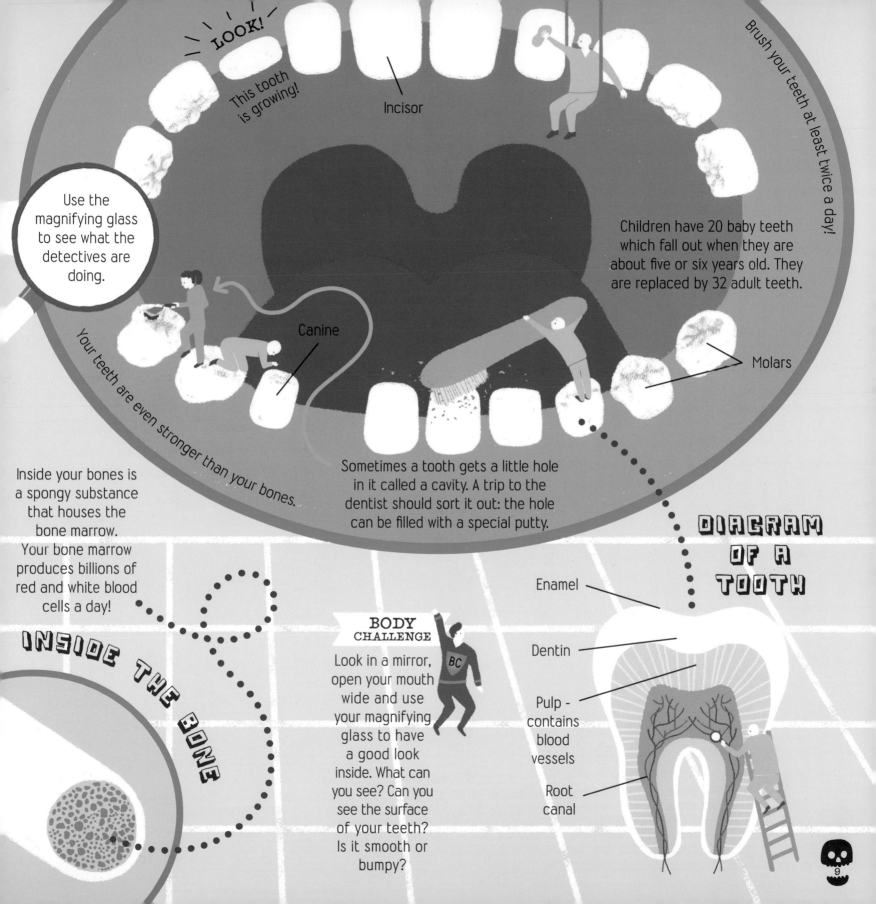

LOOK!

This tooth is growing!

Incisor

Use the magnifying glass to see what the detectives are doing.

Children have 20 baby teeth which fall out when they are about five or six years old. They are replaced by 32 adult teeth.

Your teeth are even stronger than your bones.

Canine

Molars

Inside your bones is a spongy substance that houses the bone marrow. Your bone marrow produces billions of red and white blood cells a day!

Sometimes a tooth gets a little hole in it called a cavity. A trip to the dentist should sort it out: the hole can be filled with a special putty.

DIAGRAM OF A TOOTH

Enamel

INSIDE THE BONE

BODY CHALLENGE

Look in a mirror, open your mouth wide and use your magnifying glass to have a good look inside. What can you see? Can you see the surface of your teeth? Is it smooth or bumpy?

Dentin

Pulp - contains blood vessels

Root canal

9

BRAIN

The brain is your body's central command station — like a computer it stores and processes information. It helps you to talk, to work out the answers to maths questions and, most importantly it tells the rest of your body what to do.

FRONTAL LOBE

This is the hub of the brain where you think and make decisions.

MEMORIES

Q

What's a decision?

A

Well, would you like to have a sandwich for lunch or a bowl of soup? That's a decision for you to make!

Use your magnifying glass to see what is happening in the brain.

Your brain is like a library that stores all your experiences and knowledge.

I think it's great!

I disagree..

Who am I?

Chocolate is good for you! The smell of it sends signals to your brain that can make you feel relaxed.

10

LEARNING HEAD

Here is where your brain processes numbers, letters and maps.

AMAZING NERVES!

If you stepped on a pin, nerves in your skin would detect the pain and send signals to your brain at lightening speed telling you to remove the pin.

EYE SPY

This part of your brain makes sense of what you see, including recognizing different colours and shapes.

DREAMS!

When you fall asleep your body is resting but your brain doesn't switch off. The parts linked to imagination and creativity remain active.

BALANCE!

This part of your brain keeps you upright and helps you co-ordinate your movements!

MUSCLES

Muscles are not just about strength. You need them to move every part of your body from your toes to your face. Muscles work by transferring energy into movement. We usually think of muscles as the ones we can see in our arms and legs. In fact, they are everywhere in your body, from your eyes to your internal organs.

MIGHTY MUSCLE FACT FILE

SMALL BUT MIGHTY
the strongest muscles are the ones surrounding your eyes.

BUSIEST MUSCLE
is somewhere on this page... Can you find it?

LONGEST MUSCLE
runs from the outside of the hip down to the inside of the knee.

SMALLEST MUSCLE
is in your ear.

LARGEST MUSCLE
is actually in your bottom!

(ooh, I say!)

Without muscles, we couldn't move at all!

Try moving very slowly and you may be able to feel different muscles doing their job. Think about every part of your body that needs muscles to move.

The ones in your arms are called skeletal muscles. They help you to move and you control them with your brain.

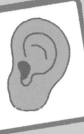

Muscles are a lot like elastic. They are made of fibres that stretch and relax to help you move.

SKELETAL MUSCLES

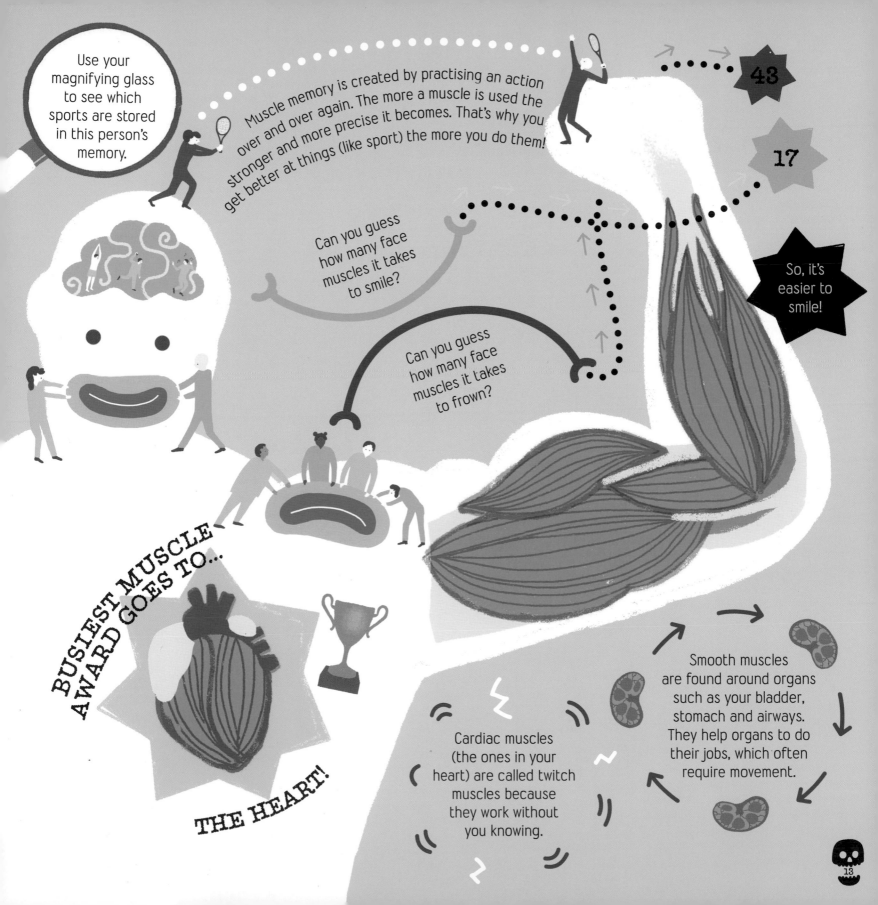

NOSE AND EARS

Senses are ways in which your body helps you to enjoy the world around you — through smell, taste, hearing, sight and touch. Can you imagine what it would be like not to be able to smell or taste things? Or not to see or hear?

THE HAIRY GATES

WHAT IS SNOT?

Your nose is full of tiny hairs that help to remove dirt and pollen from the air that you breathe in.

CLEVER NOSES!

Your nose can smell nice smells, bad smells and warn you of dangerous smells — like harmful chemicals!

Snot helps to warm the air that comes into your nose.

Snot also catches dust and bacteria that could irritate your lungs. Pretty amazing stuff!

SNEEZES
AH CHOO!

Sneezes are fast, they can travel at 100 miles an hour — as fast as a racing car!

A sneeze releases around 100,000 germs into the air (so better catch it with a tissue or they will go everywhere)!

TASTE EXPERIMENT

Try eating some of your favourite food while holding your nose. Tastes different, doesn't it? That's because most of your taste is done by smelling food! Try eating different foods blindfolded and pinching your nose. Can you guess what they are?

To learn about sight, turn over the page!

The smallest bones can be found in your ear.

Use your magnifying glass to see which is the smallest bone.

This is the smallest bone

No no this is the tiniest

The smallest is less than a centimetre long.

Your ears are more than just necessary for hearing; they also help you keep your balance.

Your sense of hearing relies on tiny hairs deep inside your ears. Without these, you couldn't hear.

Sound waves like this one travel to your ear and are changed into nerve impulses which are sent to the brain. Your brain understands this as sound.

Ear wax may seem disgusting but it is your body's way of keeping your ears clean. Don't mess with it; let it do its work!

DON'T FORGET TO WASH BEHIND YOUR EARS!

MYTH BUSTER

If your eyes are open when you sneeze they will pop out of your head.
Not true! Your eyes close when we sneeze to stop the germs getting in (the ones you have just sneezed out!), not to keep your eyes in.

TASTE

WAR OF THE BOGIES!

Oh yes we will

I'm free!

No, you will not get past us

As gruesome as bogies are, they are very important in the fight to stop horrible germs and bacteria getting into your body. You see, germs and bacteria try to get through your nose but end up getting stuck inside this gloop and then blown out later.

15

EYES

Your eyes are amazing organs allowing you to see the world around you. Why do you have two of them? If you only had one you would see things in two dimensions rather than three, making everything look flat!

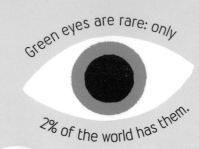

Green eyes are rare: only 2% of the world has them.

About 8% of the world has blue eyes.

EYE COLOUR
is determined by melanin. The more you have, the darker your eyes.

About 8% of the world has hazel eyes.

Did you know some people have two different coloured eyes? This is called Heterochromia!

Brown eyes are the most common. Over 50% of the world has brown eyes.

IRIS

PUPIL

CORNEA

Eating carrots makes you see in the dark. Not true BUT carrots do contain lots of vitamin A, which can help improve your eyesight!

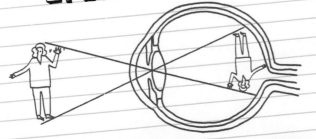

UPSIDE DOWN!

The human eye actually sees everything upside down! The images then travel to the brain, which turns them the right way up.

Use your magnifying glass to look closely at your eyes in a mirror. Can you see blood vessels?

BODY CHALLENGE

What colour eyes have you got? What about the people around you? Can you find anyone with green eyes?

CROCODILE TEARS

Not all tears are because we feel sad or in pain. The body uses tears as a way of cleaning the eye. Have you ever noticed that when you get a bit of dust in your eye it starts watering? This is your body's way of flushing out unwelcome dirt.

DIAGRAM OF THE EYE

To the brain →

COLOUR BLINDNESS
Males are much more likely to be colour blind than females. The most common problem is telling red from green.

DID YOU KNOW?
The pupil is black because it is actually a hole behind the lens!

Have a go at our colour blind test!

See if you can see the shape in the middle. If you can, you are not colour blind!

17

HAIR

All mammals have hair on their bodies. Humans have a lot of hair on their head and a fine layer on their bodies. Your hair protects you in many ways. It stops the sun burning your head and keeps your temperature stable when it is either hot or cold outside. Hair comes in all different colours, shapes and lengths.

A SINGLE HAIR

skin

cuticle

cortex

follicle

medulla

Pigment is responsible for hair colours but your hair dresser can create many more! Changing your hairstyle is a fun way to express yourself!

REDHEAD
86,000 hairs

BLONDE
146,000 hairs

BLACK
110,000 hairs

People with blonde hair normally have more hairs on their head!

MYTH BUSTER

Cutting will help it grow faster... Not true! Your hair grows about 1cm per month but this can be affected by what you eat and drink.

Eyebrows and eyelashes . . .

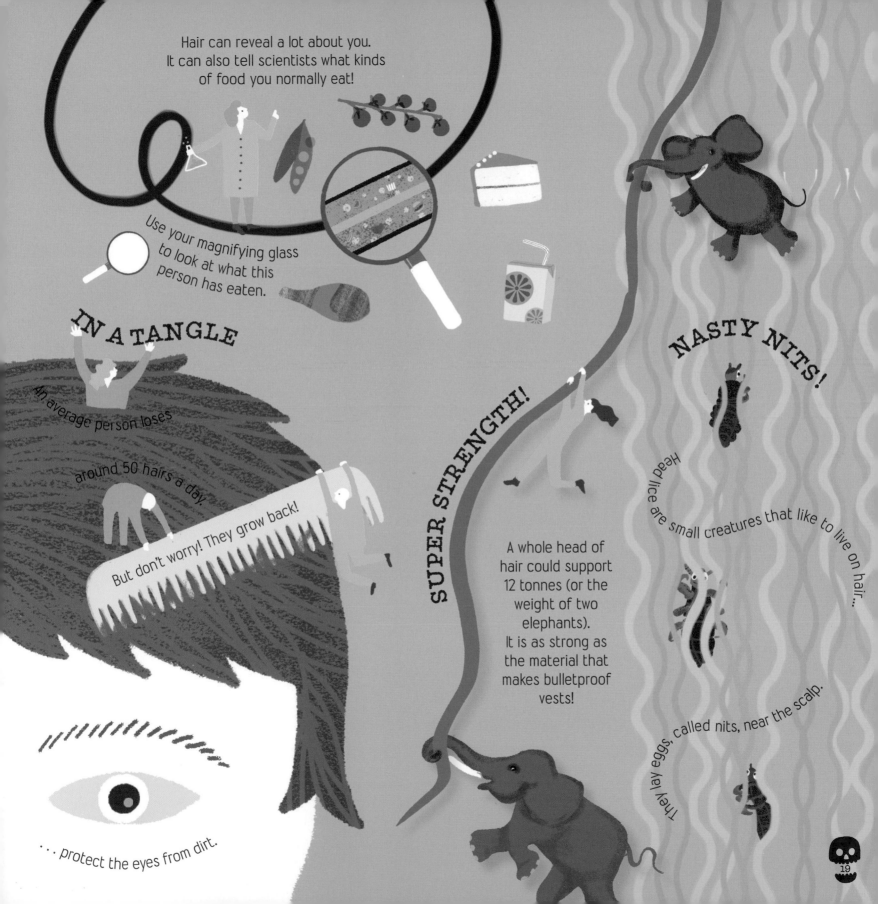

Hair can reveal a lot about you. It can also tell scientists what kinds of food you normally eat!

Use your magnifying glass to look at what this person has eaten.

IN A TANGLE

An average person loses around 50 hairs a day.

But don't worry! They grow back!

...protect the eyes from dirt.

SUPER STRENGTH!

A whole head of hair could support 12 tonnes (or the weight of two elephants). It is as strong as the material that makes bulletproof vests!

NASTY NITS!

Head lice are small creatures that like to live on hair...

They lay eggs, called nits, near the scalp.

SKIN

Your skin is an amazing organ. It covers your entire body and holds everything together! Without it your other organs, bones and muscles would hang all over the place. It also provides a waterproof barrier against outside nasties!

Your skin contains a chemical called melanin — the more you have the darker your skin.

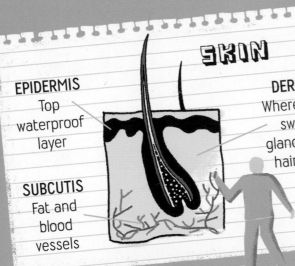

SKIN

EPIDERMIS
Top waterproof layer

DERMIS
Where your sweat glands and hairs live

SUBCUTIS
Fat and blood vessels

Melanin is also responsible for your eye colour.

If you didn't have any skin, your organs would fall out of your body and you would evaporate!

GOOSE PIMPLES

WHY? WHY? WHY? WHY?

When you are cold, the small muscles attached to each hair follicle get tight. This makes your hairs stand up straight creating goose pimples!

TOUCH EXPERIMENT

How much can you 'see' with your hands? Place different objects in boxes and ask a friend to feel the objects without looking at them. Can they guess what they are? Touch is a very powerful sense!

TO THE BRAIN

There are thousands of nerve endings in your skin. They help you feel hot, cold and pain.

These nerves endings send messages to your brain, telling you to react to the situation.

HEALTHY SKIN CHECKLIST!

A Vitamin A helps treat sunburn!

C Vitamin C for sun protection!

E Vitamin E for anti-aging!

D Vitamin D for spot prevention!

BIGGEST ORGAN AWARD GOES TO... SKIN!!

Did you know? If you stretched your skin out it would cover about two square metres! That's about the size of a big bed.

21

WASTE FACTORY

Everybody wees, poos, burps, trumps and hiccups and is sick sometimes. These are all wonderfully natural bodily functions.

WHY DO WE SWEAT?

What is sweat? Sweat is the body's way of cooling itself down. For example, if you exercise you get hot and you may start to sweat to bring your temperature back to a comfortable level.

BURP!

Burping releases gas that has built up in your body from swallowing air. You might not know it, but you swallow air all the time — especially when you eat or talk quickly, chew gum, or drink through a straw.

HICCUP!

You probably had your first experience of hiccups before you were born. Babies often get hiccups inside their mum's tummy!

Your stomach stores the food you eat. It is full of special acidic juices that break your chewed food down into a liquid mixture.

Vomiting is your body's way of forcing out nasties. stomach acids which gives it a strong smell and colour! It contains

Eating beetroot can change the colour of your wee (to purple, obviously) and eating asparagus may make it smell.

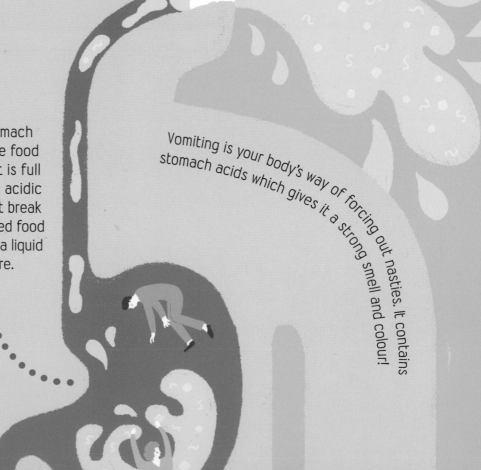

You wee about 6.3 cups a day!

STOMACH

LARGE INTESTINE

SMALL INTESTINE

KIDNEY

KIDNEY

About 75% if your poo is water. If you don't drink enough it may be hard to poo!

The first man to walk on the moon, Neil Armstrong, left samples of poo and wee up there...!

WHY DOES POO SMELL?
It is full of bacteria that produce very smelly gasses!

DON'T HOLD IT IN

GO ON, MAKE A DIN!

toot toot
PUMP!
bottom burp
PARP! PARP! PARP!
backdoor trumpet

Trumping is your body's way of getting rid of unwanted gasses and we do this about 14 times a day!

BLADDER

URETHRA
Where the wee comes out.

ANUS
Where the poo comes out.

The world's longest poo was 26 feet!

MYTH BUSTER
Wee helps with a jellyfish sting. Not true! It will make it worse.

BODY CHALLENGE
Next time you do a poo, see what type it is...
BC

BRISTOL STOOL CHART

Type 3 — Like a sausage but with cracks on its surface.

Type 1 — Separate hard lumps, like nuts. Hard to poo.

Type 4 — Like a sausage or snake, smooth and soft.

Type 2 — Sausage-shaped but lumpy.

Type 5 — Soft blobs with clear-cut edges.

Type 7 — Watery, no solid pieces... (yukky!)

Type 6 — Fluffy pieces with ragged edges.

23

REPAIR ZONE

Sometimes we have accidents and hurt ourselves (oops!). Whether you have broken a leg, or just got a little graze on your knee, your body works to fix itself.

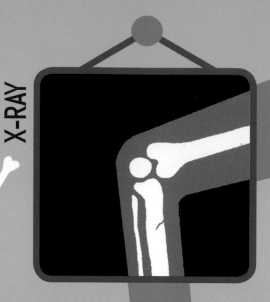

X-RAY

FRACTURE ZONE

Bones can break in many different ways!

OPEN FRACTURE

Where the bone breaks and pokes through the skin. **Yuk!**

SINGLE FRACTURE

When the bone is broken in one place, like a chip.

COMPLETE FRACTURE

When a bone is broken into two pieces.

BOWING FRACTURE

When the bone bends but doesn't actually break; this usually only happens to children.

X-RAY

Almost everyone will break their small toe bones in their life time but there is nothing you can do but wait for it to heal!

SCABS

A scab is your body's own version of a plaster. It stops germs getting in and allows the skin underneath to heal. New skin cells are made and the damage can be repaired. When the skin has finished healing the scab will fall off!

DID YOU KNOW

A scab is a protective crust of dried blood that forms over a cut to help it during healing.

DON'T PICK SCABS!

If you do, you may be left with a scar because the skin will have to start healing all over again!

GERMS + MICROBES

Use your magnifying glass to look at the germs? Can you spot the tiny ones?

WHAT HAPPENS UNDER A SCAB?

YOUR AMAZING BODY

Once you've had a germ, your body remembers it and is protected against it in the future.

WAR ZONE!

Your body is like a fortress, ready to fight off any invaders.

Take that!

25

HOW WE GROW

As you get older you get bigger and taller. Your bones stretch and your weight increases. Other body changes happen too: you lose your baby teeth and get new adult ones, voices get deeper and during puberty you gain a lot more hair!

MYTH BUSTER

Hanging from your arms will make you taller. Not true!

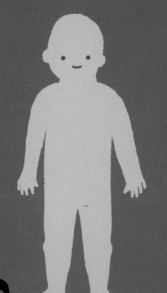

In the first year of your life you grow the fastest you'll ever grow (an amazing 25 cm)! That's about the length of this book!

After age 2, you will probably grow about 6 cm a year.

As a teenager you will experience a second growth spurt. For girls, this is between 8 and 13 years old; for boys, between 10 and 15 years old.

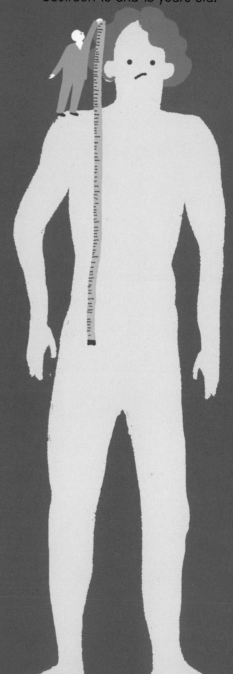

MAKE A GROWTH CHART

A fun thing to do is to record your height and weight in a growth chart. Take an exercise book and write down your height and weight every month for a year!

26

Between 18 and 21 years you will stop growing.

FOODS WHICH HELP US GROW

Milk for healthy bones

Spinach for strength

Fish and beans for protein

Fruit and vegetables for vitamins

DID YOU KNOW?

You are slightly taller in the morning than when you go to bed at night. This is because your spine gets squashed during the day. When you lie in bed your spine relaxes and it spreads out!

You could also draw around your hands and feet to see how much they grow!

Zzz

Good sleep is important in helping you to grow. In fact, you do most of your growing during the night hours. Growing is a complicated business though you will also need to eat well and exercise.

Zzz

Everybody needs a different amount of sleep, but here's the average number of hours:
Baby — 16 hours or so a day
2-5 year olds — 10-12 hours
6-12 year olds — 9.5-11.5 hours
13+ — 8 hours

SWEET DREAMS

ACTIVITIES

Now that you have explored every nook and cranny of our body, it's time to turn the magnifying glass on yourself and see what you can find!

Next time no one is watching, have a good rummage around your nose and see what interesting treats you can find. Put them on a white piece of paper and have a good look at them under your magnifying glass.

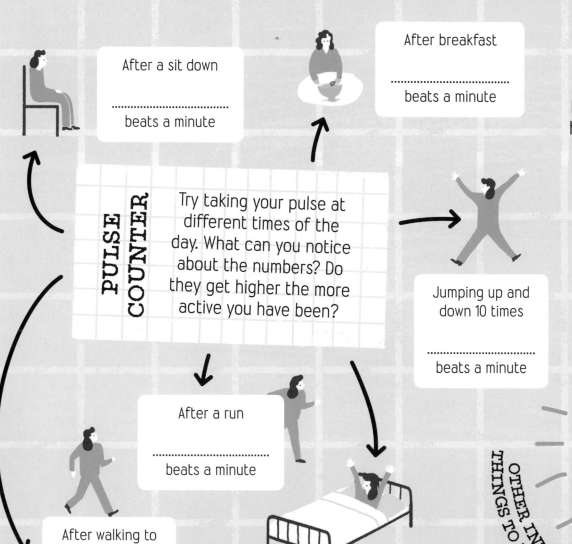

After a sit down

....

beats a minute

After breakfast

....

beats a minute

PULSE COUNTER

Try taking your pulse at different times of the day. What can you notice about the numbers? Do they get higher the more active you have been?

Jumping up and down 10 times

....

beats a minute

After a run

....

beats a minute

After walking to school

....

beats a minute

Early in the morning

....

beats a minute

OTHER INTERESTING THINGS TO DRAW AROUND

YOUR FEET   YOUR HANDS

Keep track of how these grow and change throughout a year, too.

28

FRUIT AND VEGETABLES

MEAT AND FISH

EAT WELL, LIVE WELL

A balanced diet will help you to live longer and feel healthier. Here's a guide to which food groups are the best for you.

LIQUIDS

HOW MUCH OF EACH GROUP DO YOU EAT EACH DAY?

GRAIN PRODUCTS

DAIRY PRODUCTS

RECORD YOUR OWN GROWTH CHART

DATE	HEIGHT IN CM

GLOSSARY

CIRCULATORY SYSTEM
The way that blood is transported around your body.

MOLAR
One of the large teeth towards the back of your mouth, used for chewing.

ALVEOLI
The little air bags in your lungs that transfer oxygen to your blood.

EXCRETION
A fancy name for wee and poo.

PUBERTY
The stage of life when your body becomes more like an adult's.

ANUS
The hole in your bottom where the poo comes out.

FOLLICLE
This is the base of a hair.

PULSE
A place on your body where you can feel how fast your heart is beating.

BONE MARROW
The spongy filling inside your bones where blood cells are made.

FRACTURE
A name for a break in your bones.

SALIVA
The watery liquid in your mouth.

BONES
A material in your body that supports and protects your organs.

INCISOR
A type of tooth at the front of your mouth, used for biting. You have eight in total!

URETHRA
The tube where your wee comes out.

CANINE
A type of tooth, often pointy, towards the front of your mouth, top and bottom.

MELANIN
A chemical that determines what colour your skin and eyes will be.

X-RAY
A special picture taken to look at the bones inside your body.